D0339966

HILLSBORO PUBLIC LIBRARY
Hillsboro, OR
Member of Washington County
COOPERATIVE LIBRARY SERVICES

A Note to Parents

Your child is beginning the lifelong adventure of reading! And with the **World of Reading** program, you can be sure that he or she is receiving the encouragement needed to become a confident, independent reader. This program is specially designed to encourage your child to enjoy reading at every level by combining exciting, easy-to-read stories featuring favorite characters with colorful art that brings the magic to life.

The **World of Reading** program is divided into four levels so that children at any stage can enjoy a successful reading experience:

Reader-in-Training
Pre-K–Kindergarten
Picture reading and word repetition for children who are getting ready to read.

Beginner Reader
Pre-K–Grade 1
Simple stories and easy-to-sound-out words for children who are just learning to read.

Junior Reader
Kindergarten- Grade 2
Slightly longer stories and more varied sentences perfect for children who are reading with the help of a parent.

Super Reader
Grade 1–Grade 3
Encourages independent reading with rich story lines and wide vocabulary that's right for children who are reading on their own.

Learning to read is a once-in-a-lifetime adventure, and with **World of Reading**, the journey is just beginning!

Copyright © 2013 Disney Enterprises, Inc.
All rights reserved. Published by Disney Press, an imprint of Disney Book Group. No part of this book may
be reproduced or transmitted in any form or by any means, electronic or mechanical, including photocopying,
recording, or by any information storage and retrieval system, without written permission from the publisher.
For information address Disney Press, 114 Fifth Avenue, New York, New York 10011-5690.
Printed in the United States of America
First Edition
1 3 5 7 9 10 8 6 4 2
G658-7729-4-12336
Library of Congress Catalog Card Number: 2012936872

ISBN 978-1-4231-6962-8

For more Disney Press fun, visit www.disneybooks.com

If you purchased this book without a cover, you should be aware that this book is stolen property.
It was reported as "unsold and destroyed" to the publisher, and neither the author nor the publisher
has received any payment for this "stripped" book.

SUSTAINABLE
FORESTRY
INITIATIVE
Certified Chain of Custody
Promoting Sustainable Forestry
www.sfiprogram.org
SFI-01415
The SFI label applies to the text stock

Disney

MICKEY & FRIENDS
Goofy at Bat

By Susan Amerikaner
Illustrated by the Disney Storybook Artists
and Loter, Inc.

Disney PRESS
New York

"Come one and all,
   put your skills to the test.
Try out today.
   Our new team needs the best!"

Goofy decides
he will sign up today.
He knows that his friends
can teach him to play!

"Donald, please help.
I must learn this new game.
Please be my coach.
No one else is the same!"

Goofy must learn
how to hold the bat right.
"Grip it like that,
and hold it real tight."

Mickey's pitch curves,
moving from spot to spot.
Goofy ends up
in a big Goofy knot.

Donald says, "Goof,
try to hit this one deep."
But the ball takes so long,
Goofy falls fast asleep!

Mickey winds up.
His next pitch is fast.
Goofy stands tall.
This ball will not pass!

Goofy swings hard.
The ball flies fast and low.
Coach Donald calls,
"Hurry up, run home, go!"

Goofy turns home,
and he runs straight ahead.
Donald cries out,
"Run to third base instead!"

Goofy tries catching.
He picks up his mitt.
He waits for the batter
to get her first hit.

Minnie bats first.
The ball flies toward the seats.
Goofy runs fast.
It is caught in his cleats!

Goofy can catch!
He can catch any ball!
Look at him go,
off the board, through the wall!

Donald says, "Goof,
you are sure to go far.
This is your game.
Yes, you <u>will</u> be a star!"

"You should play, too,"
Goofy says with a hyuck.
"Try out with me.
Your help brings me good luck."

Donald says, "Yes,
that is just what to do.
This game is more fun
when I play it with you."